—— CLUB ——
MOROCCO

JOHN MICHELE

PAGE PUBLISHING, INC.
Conneaut Lake, PA

First originally published by Page Publishing 2021

Author photograph courtesy of Dachowski Photography

ISBN 978-1-6624-4397-8 (pbk)
ISBN 978-1-6624-4398-5 (digital)

Printed in the United States of America

AUTHOR'S NOTE

I BELIEVE IT is important and necessary to state that my story was not taken from crime news or real events. Many of the characters were part of my extended family during my teen years, and their actual names were in fact used. Today, reality seems to cloud imagination but not destroy it. There may be some unavoidable unpleasant comparisons of a name, place, or situation. However, one cannot be held responsible for the roll of the dice, better described as chance.

ACKNOWLEDGMENTS

Living by one's self is a lonely existence, and especially during this time of COVID-19. When one's beautiful wife has passed, and children are spread all over the globe, old family stories and memories, especially the happy rewarding ones, do occupy some time. But not enough, especially if one had enjoyed a busy, productive life.

That's when my beautiful, caring friend, Joanne Gerety, whom I've known for almost twenty years, said to me one day, "John, you write very well. You should have your stories and ideas put to paper in book form."

The only writing I've done in past years was writing advertising copy and providing annual reports to bank regulators, the SEC, and stockholder, which were reviewed by attorneys and CPAs before seeing the light of day. I never believed I had the ability to write fiction, but here I am!

Thank you, Joanne Gerety, for being here when it was needed and welcomed. Your ideas, suggestions, and, yes, pushing me to do better than my best has resulted in the publication of *Club Morocco*.

My 102-year-old aunt, Rose Connelly, sharp as a tack, with a strong memory to boot, was there the day I was born at home and has provided much accurate, colorful, at times salty, descriptions of life back during the '30s, '40s, and '50s that existed during the days of Club Morocco. I call her each week, and we cheer up each other in remembering good pastimes, our big Sicilian family, and all the love we shared during those great days.

I live in a beautiful neighborhood. It is the people living here that make it so. A special thank you to Dina Delisle and Elaine

Petersen, my proofreaders and givers of constructive criticism. They are a joy to be with. My daughter-in-law, Karin Bates, fits into the same mold as my neighbors. To my friend Paul Remus, I owe you for more than your friendship.

Lastly, my four children, Stephen, Joseph, Patrice, and Susan, were startled, proud, I think, and I'm sure surprised to learn that their old dad was going to be a published author. So am I.

HISTORY

The Outhouse

"Sally, why are you pressing me for information? You know you arc, and I hate that my past always seems to keep popping up. It just follows me everywhere."

"You know why. After reading about you finding that body in the mud near the outhouse, as described in the news stories, I must dig deeper into your past. There is a story there waiting to be told."

"Now, Professor Sally Marshall, I'm one of your writing students in your literature class, and I know you're using me with that sweet body to get what you want. Look at you, one would think you're twenty-five, but you're not. You're blond, blue-eyed, and have a hard sexy body, like that professional tennis player limbering up. Are you giving me *As* for my writing or what? Really, what's going on?"

"Forget my age, John Boy, that is how they describe you in the *Globe* story."

"I know, won't live that down either."

"Come on, give me some information."

"If you insist, but you will pay one way or another. Okay, Sally, let me tell you about one of the central characters in that *Globe* story."

"Who is that?"

"He's that son of a bitch, the chief of police Oscar Bates. He was chief of police for at least twenty-five years before I came into his sights, or him in mine. Must have been a big handsome guy when young. When he and I met, he was older, tall, with thinning gray hair, kinda fat, probably 225 pounds or so. Married young when he was new to the force, and people, from what I was told, took to him. Always had a line of bullshit that he used on anyone he could. His wife died giving birth, and the baby did not survive. From that point on, he was a different person. I was told he had his eye on the chief's position from his first day on the force, and once there, used it for his personal benefit."

"I guess you never appreciated him."

"What do you think—I'll give you more later."

"No, tell me more now."

"My, you are a pushy dame."

"His reputation became that of a woman chaser who would go after any women—I mean any women, even younger girls, anyone good-looking and willing. Some even suggested he liked young boys. Always had plenty of money to spend, and when young, I was told to stay clear of him. I first met him when I first did little jobs for one of my uncles. That's when the story in the *Globe* really started to develop. It happened like this."

"Johnny, it's close to opening time, so let's get this place ready."

"Yeah, Uncle Jim, I will, but first need to use stinking outhouse. It's all mud out there with the spring rainstorms. I won't be long." "I'd usually just go behind a big tree, not this time."

"Boy, that place always smelled like a pile of chicken shit and that's why it's twenty-five yards away. I hate this fuckin' job. If my mom heard me, I would catch hell. She wasn't happy about me being here, especially at my age, but we can use money later for college, if I ever get there. But cleaning all the shit on the floor left by the players at the club was almost as disgusting as the outhouse."

Speaking of hell, what is that covered with bushes near the out-house? Holy shit, it looks like a man's body facedown in the mud. It is…

The back of the head looks bashed in, and bugs and worms are all over dried blood. The fingers are dug into the mud as if it is trying to get up.

"Sally, I forgot to pee and ran back to the shack."

"Jimmy, Jimmy, there's a dead body in the mud out by the outhouse."

"Is this one of your tricks?"

"No, no, there is a dead body out there."

"When my uncle saw it, he said the same."

"Holy shit. Run down the hill to your great-uncle's Carlo's place. It's the white house set back with red shutters and a red door. Just where the pavement ends on Stark Avenue. Tell him what we saw and to call the police."

"I'll run, it's about a half mile from here. But, Uncle Jim, I know the place from when I was about five years old, especially during Christmas."

"As I ran, even with the body in the mud, I could not help going back to the Christmas family gatherings. I knew my great-grandfather. At five-foot-two, it was without hesitation; everyone knew he was the head of our Sicilian clan. Everyone called him Papanonno. His six children, three sons and three daughters, with their husbands and wives, their children and great-grandchildren were all expected to spend a part of the day at his place. The aroma of Sicilian foods and desserts and the music, plus homemade wine, combined for lively days."

"Giovanni, come here, so I can show you where I keep your Christmas gift."

"Sure, Papanonno," I said as I followed him to his special closet.

"See, inside I have a small vault. I'm the only one who has the combination so don't tell anyone what you see."

"What are you taking out?"

"This little cloth bag has the coins I will give to you and all of your cousins."

"He again locked the vault and began to give two dimes to each kid. A dime is not much, but during the Second World War, it was enough for a kid to attend a movie and leave some pennies for candy. The movies were afternoon long with double features and updates about World War II. Sally, I will never forget those days and how safe and how much love there was for everyone."

"John, get back to the body in the woods."
"If I must."

"They arrived in twenty minutes."
"Has anyone been near the body?"
"Don't think so, Dan," Jimmy and I said at the same time.
"Who found the body?"
"The kid, John."
"Where is he?"
"I'm in the outhouse taking a piss."
"The cop was Detective Dan Devine, a longtime officer on our police force. He carefully turned the body over."
"Oh my god…"
"Devine turned white, looked like he was about to lose it. The sight of all that dried blood must have got to him. Then he said, *'Get everyone out of the crime area and into the shack. Jimmy, I need a list of everyone who was here last night. I mean everyone, including the players and all your people.'*"
"It suddenly came to me that my sweeping days were over, and the casino in the woods was as dead as the body in the mud."

CHAPTER 1

Protection

"HERE HE COMES *looking for his protection money. That chief badge is always there to show everyone who's the boss. Without it, he is naked, walks in like he owns the place. Bastard!*"

"*Look at him pushing past others in line.*"

"*Mary, two of your best prime steaks, two pounds of sweet sausage, one pound of hamburger, and I'll use the shelves for everything else.*"

"*Okay, Chief, it'll take a while.*" *Mary was my grandmother's sister. A smart, efficient businesswoman who ran a profitable corner grocery store.*

"*In my mind, I can just hear Dolf.*"

"*That son of a bitch thinks he is God's gift to women, telling everyone he is the 'professor of love' like the poet Ovid during the time of the Roman Empire. Where the hell did he ever learn about the poet writer Ovid? Must be smarter than one would expect. When he saw me back here, his attitude changed. He's a big man, but if he ever made a play for Mary, I'd take him apart. Even the officers in his force keep their wives, daughters, and even their sons as far away as they can.*"

"*Hurry up, Chief, I don't want the paying customers to see what is going on.*"

"*Don't rush me, Dolf, it'll get done. You know I'm very selective.*"

"*No, you're picky as hell for someone who gets a piece of my action.*"

"Dolf and the chief saw one another usually on a weekly basis in my little town of Breakheart, north of Boston. Their meetings, told to me by relatives, gave me a little view about life during the prohibition years in the late 1920s until 1933, and of hard times experienced in my immigrant neighborhood during the Depression. During that time, Dolf was operating as a small-time bootlegger and doing very well.

"I was born the same year that my great-uncle Dolf suffered a bad stroke. His wife, Mary, was my grandmother's sister. Mary and Dolf carried half of the neighborhood on their books when neighbors were short on money. It was a close-knit community. I saw little of Dolf until after World War Two, and even then, it was just for short visits. I remember a time when he was at Uncle Jimmy's goodbye get-together before he left for service in 1943. Dolf always said 'Stare bene, Giovanni,' meaning 'Be well, Giovanni.'

"Dolf had great, big soft hands, like a baseball glove. He was a great big bear of a man weighing in at 350 pounds. His eyes were clear and bright, with a ruddy face. For a man of six feet five, he was light and quick on his feet. He and Mary didn't have their own kids. He just loved all of the kids in the neighborhood. On nice warm days, he would pile as many as would fit in his cab and in the back of his old 1930s Ford pickup and slowly drive them all over town.

"Never took a drink with kids on board, but if he started on his own booze, he just didn't stop with a few. Then he was so hard to control that everyone just stayed away for their own safety. He at times would say, 'Everyone has problems, even me.' That's when his temper took over.

"The chief of police was Oscar Bates. Many years later, I asked my dad's sister, Rose, a sharp 102-year-old with vivid memory, for anything she remembered about Bates. 'You mean that bastard who shopped for free every week at Mary's store? He was always on the take.' Same words that Dolf used. I wondered how many of these type arrangements were going on across town.

"My dad was in Mary's store one day and told me of a meeting-of-minds talk between the chief and Dolf that he witnessed from a little distance. It went like this.

"Chief, I see you looking at Mary's ass. If you ever put a hand on her, it will be a sorry day for you."

"Dolf, are you threatening me?"

"Bates, I'll bet there are quite a few guys in this town who hate your guts. As for me, I know people who would love to break your legs, just for the fun of it. If I were you, I would always be watching my back."

"Dolf, we have a business relationship, let's keep it at that."

"Fine with me, just the way I want it."

"Somehow, I ended up with Dolf's framed picture. It was easy to see he was a massive man. No one ever tried to physically get the best of Dolf even after his stroke. His real name was Adolf, and for obvious reasons, he shortened it in 1939 after the invasion of Poland. He was a good guy, as I said, a small-time bootlegger who would not, at times, stay away from his own product. Every place he went, Dolf drew a crowd. Each week, he would drive to the open-air market in Boston's North End for supplies for Mary's store and for his bootlegging operation which lasted until 1933. One day, a wrestling promoter, Paul Bowser, witnessed Dolf carrying a barrel of olives on his shoulder and offered to promote him as Mountain Man. 'Not my cup of tea,' he told Bowser. All that did was enhance his reputation for massive strength and served to let the chief and all others know just who they were dealing with.

"It was said that Dolf told Bates to never in any way go after the wife of a Sicilian or any of his family members. When it came to Dolf and Mary, Bates got the message. But during prohibition, protection payments continued. 'Remember, Dolf, business is business!' These old family stories, told to me by my dad and his brothers and sisters, were a heritage gift that I didn't appreciate at the time.

"My contact with Oscar Bates didn't happen until I was about thirteen years old, a few years after World War II was over. That's when I asked my aunt about him 'cause he seemed kind of strange toward me and others, especially attractive young women."

"Uncle Jimmy, can you tell me why the big cop, the chief of police, keeps coming here every week, usually on Monday afternoon?"

"When you're a little older, I'll fill you in, but for now just keep your distance from him."

"But why?"

"Hope you never find out—not now, the players are starting to arrive. Time for you to help." I knew why he kept showing up, just wanted to know if I was right.

"My uncle Jim, Jimmy, looked like an Italian movie star. He was not as big, about five-foot-eight, with dark somewhat curly hair, light skin, after his mom, my grandmother, with flashing eyes that picked up everything that was going on around him. His formal education ended after about grade nine, I think the first year of high school, but he was smart and educated himself about the way things work in this world. He was an easy touch for friends and family. Even paid the funeral expenses for a friend, an American Indian, who didn't have a dime to his name. To me, his big problem was he liked to gamble thinking it was the way to riches. Physically, he was tough as nails and knew how to take care of himself and his family, if needed."

"Can you tell me about your time in North Africa during World War II?"

"I guess so. In fact, when I was there, my ideas about this place jelled in my head. Never believed I would use them, but here I am."

CHAPTER 2

A Smart Kid

"Uncle Jimmy, what was Operation Torch?"

"Oh, John Boy, I see you have been doing a little reading about World War II, am I right?"

"Yeah, you are. I wanted to learn a little about the time you spent in North Africa and Sicily. You said you would tell me about your time in the US Army Air Force."

"So come on, tell me, your brother John has little to say."

"Well, he saw much more action than I did with General Patton's army tank divisions. Even was in the battle of the Bulge area of France. Did I ever tell you how he captured three hundred Germans without firing a shot? That's another story for later. Better yet, ask Uncle John. He was there, not me."

"What about North Africa? Tell me."

"Well, here is just a little. Operation Torch began before I arrived by about three or four months. It was the name given for the invasion of North African countries of Morocco, Algeria, and Tunisia by the western Allies, mostly by the troops from the United States and Great Britain and some from Canada. I landed in the late winter at Casablanca and saw action all across North Africa and served in the US Army Air Corps as part of the ground crew."

"Uncle Jimmy, did you see action?"

"Only when we grew closer to Algeria and Tunisia. That is when the German fighters and bombers were able to attack us. We had to duck into ditches and behind anything for protection. I can remember praying, 'God, if you're up there, get me the hell out of here in one piece.'"

"I thought you didn't believe in God?"

"On those attack nights, it was different."

"What did you all do when there was no air strikes or at night?"

"Fight off the bugs and snakes and play cards and enjoying the down time, but mostly not worrying about German fighter planes. Getting beer was always a problem, and usually it was warm as piss—we drank it anyway. We knew we were making slow progress across North Africa 'cause we began seeing graffiti signs, 'Kilroy was here.' No one knows who Kilroy was, but all the GIs loved the signs. They meant we were getting to the Krauts. The first one I saw was in Tunisia, before the invasion of Sicily. That's where your grandparents, my parents, came from."

"I know, Santa Caterina Villa Mosa. I asked Pa about his hometown. Did you see the town?"

"Came close, but no I didn't. The invasion of Sicily only took only a little better than one month during July and August to drive the Germans out. They didn't even have time to rip up train tracks, and we used them to get our infantry across the island to Massina near the toe of Italy. John, have you ever seen your grandparents, Ma and Pa, put their fingers to their mouths and say, 'Don't talk about what happened at the farm in Sicily'?"

"Yeah, why do they do that?"

"Well, don't you ever repeat this story, 'cause sometimes very bad unexpected things happen during war."

"I was riding in a troop train and noticed this officer, a captain, as I remember, poking his gun out the window and shooting at young Sicilian farm workers, young like you and your brother. All I could think about was all of my nephews and nieces back in America about the same ages. It was bullshit and wanted to turn the gun on him. Instead, when the train stopped at night, near a small farm, I asked if I could speak privately with him. He was from out West, Oklahoma, I think. Spoke with a western twang. I told him just how I felt. He took a swing at me, *yelling that he was a captain and I was a lowly private and that I should shut up about what he does or does not do.*

"His bad mistake. I beat the living hell out of him. In the courtyard of this farm, while the fight was happening, we were being watched by a couple of workers. I could speak Sicilian Italian and explained why we were fighting and how the captain was shooting at young Sicilians. Putting their fingers to their mouths, they politely asked me to leave. As I was going back to the train, I could see they were picking the captain up and then dumped him down a deep well. I don't know what happened, but just maybe, somewhere in Sicily, the bones of that guy are at the bottom of a well. That's war!"

"I'll never say a word."

"Good don't. As Ma's brothers, my uncles, always said to me, 'Don't ever do harm to the family of Sicilians, they never forget.'"

"My dad said that because you spoke Italian, the army brass, as the war in Italy continued, sent you to Rome as an interpreter. Is that right?"

"Yeah, it is, but funny. I could not understand the Romans, and they couldn't understand me. My interpreter stint was very short, but Rome was not bombed during the war, and I found it beautiful. Your great-uncle Charlie goes back every year and sends postcards from all over writing his interesting comments about where he visited. Gotta talk with Charlie. Do it, he loves all of Italy.

"Visit when you are older. You will love the ancient history, the old buildings, and especially the Roman Forum and the St Peter's. And the Carrara marble statues by Michelangelo are so magnificent they made me cry for their lifelike beauty.

"Then I was on a troopship across the Atlantic Ocean and found myself in Panama Canal headed to the Pacific to fight the Japs. The war ended before I ever got there. That is where my idea started to jell about a gambling club. Nothing else to do but play cards on a troopship. Say, John Boy, when I get this club up and running, I could use a smart kid to do things. Wanna try? I'll pay you a few bucks."

"Sure, why not."

"Ask your mom first."

CHAPTER 3

A Quick Buck

"WHERE YOU GONNA get the money to do that? You said all you've had are little part-time jobs since you returned from the war."

"Johnny Boy, I've saved some of that money from those jobs, not much, but I still have my service pay that I put aside. I also told you I've had this idea in my head for some time. And I have a bookie friend, Nate, who will lend me some dough. He believes it'll work, at least long enough to pay him back, I hope. Life's a gamble.

"As I said I'm gonna open a small casino off in the woods in an old shack off the beaten path. Its tar paper on the outside but clean inside with windows and entrance in the back where they will not be seen, and it has electricity and a wood stove for heat."

"Uncle Jim, what was it used for in the past?"

"Carlo built it for some of the animals he raised, like chickens, and even some goats. He told me that it is now clean and has not been used for years, but just to be safe, keep the windows open while you are just getting ready to open and it should smell fine after a while. Besides, most of these former GI players won't know the difference given how they lived and played during the war.

"I won't advertise the name, but how about, between you and me, we call it Club Morocco? There is an area just a little away for cars to park so they won't be seen, and the trees hide the shack from view, and we're way off the beaten path, and it's half a mile up Stark Avenue where the pavement ends. I think it might work, at least until I can build a bundle of dough."

"I like the name, but how will you pull this off?"

"Well, first, now that you are a teenager, you're big and strong, and I could use a little help. I can pay you, but it will not be much, at least until I get this place up and producing some cash. Keep this location to yourself."

"No problem, I won't say a word."

"If I can keep it quiet so neighbors who are long distances away do not hear voices, I think it will work. Buying the gambling equipment is the easy part for it will be mostly card tables and chairs and a roulette wheel. And I know just the guys to man the tables, for a little cut."

"Can you trust them?"

"I think so, but we'll keep a close eye on things. Maybe you can help with that too?"

"I don't know, never did this before."

"Just tell me if something looks funny."

"Who will be the players?"

"Ex-service men will probably be most of the players, and the word will get around about a game in the woods each night. I know GIs and how they like to gamble. That's all we did at night all across North Africa."

"Uncle Jimmy, the place looks like a dump, and it's hot as hell during the day."

"I know, but most of the gambling will be at night. The trees will help, and guess I should buy some fans. Gotta try, this is my chance to get rich quick. Your great-uncles, your grandmother's brothers, live down the road away and said they would keep their eye on the place when I'm not around. Charlie travels a lot, as you know, but Sal and Carlo are usually around. Go down and say hello, I'm sure they will be happy to see you. Besides, they know what I'm doing and helped me with this shack. I'll pay them for electricity and any other expenses 'cause they own the place."

"Later that week, just after Club Morocco opened, I went to visit my great-uncles. I bumped into Chief Oscar Bates who was talking with Sal. Carlo was out in the back, framing some new building he was working on, but near enough so he could hear Sal and Bates talking. It was a heated conversation. Every time I saw Bates, he gave me the creeps.

"Bates left, and Carlo came to me and gave me a big hug."

"Giovanni, you're getting big."

"Not as big as you, Carlo."

"Carlo was a big tough man with strong hands. Sal was the smart, intellectual one, a math major in his college days."

"When you're up with Jimmy in the woods, come by for a hug."

"I will, Carlo." Then he and Sal talked about Bates.

"Carlo was the youngest and bigger than his two brothers. Like Jimmy, he had dark somewhat curly hair, but a dark ruddy complexion and a big straight Roman nose and always greeted me with a big hug. Imagine, during the later part of World War II, at age forty-six, he was drafted, went through a tough basic training with ease, never saw action 'cause the war was over before he had to. He was excellent working with his hands and enjoyed his job at the public works department in town. He kept their house in tip-top shape like he was trying to attract a woman. At least that's what Jimmy told me. Never happened.

"There was a lot of 'that pain in the ass and even more' in their talk. As I was leaving, Sal said, *"If you were just a little older, I'd give you a little of Dolf's wine, maybe next time."*

"A sip wouldn't hurt, but next time, Sal."

Then they began talking about the chief again. I always knew that these three Sicilian great-uncles, family, would always have my back.

CHAPTER 4

Up and Running

"THE WORD WAS out, and this hot spot was jumping. Ex GIs filled the place at night, bringing friends and booze along. Just as Jimmy said, the house came out the winner, and even after paying the table guys, he quickly paid his debt to Nate the bookie. And every week, usually on Monday, a certain chief would arrive for his cut or take, as Jimmy described it."

"John Boy, it's just part of life, but I hate that SOB. He always is asking for more than I want to part with."

"Sally, here I am with my uncle, just in my teen years and watching things that most kids never will see. Plus I picked up a few bucks to boot."

"John, you are seeing the grimy side of life. I'm not going to be doing this for long, only until I build up a nest egg. It is not going to be where you should be, but learn from your time here, but don't copy what you hear and see."

"Okay, Uncle Jim."

"I learned lots, especially from the young GIs. Never did I get the hang of the roulette wheel, didn't like it anyway, pure chance, all luck. But cards, blackjack and twenty-one took some skill especially when trying not to show one's hand. Show no emotion.

"I just watched. Uncle Jimmy would not let me play. After a while, I sounded like the players, spitting, smoking, yes, in my early teens, and learning more swear words even if I didn't know their meaning. Felt grown up.

"At the end of nights, I was the cleanup specialist, and I hated that job. The place stunk of cigar smoke, spilled booze, spit, and farts. Farting took place all night long. Don't know what they ate, but whatever it was made their bodies and farts smell bad, and I mean very bad. The outhouse off in the woods was always busy. But I was able to overhear some interesting stories about our town while I watched the guys play cards."

"Jake, did you hear what happened at the police station last night? My brother Al cleans the place after hours, and he told me that the chief and his leading detective almost came to blows."

"Why?"

"Chief Bates made a play for Daniel's wife, Lilly. She is a real looker."

"Yeah, she is. Her long legs go all the way up and with her long blond hair—"

"My god, you noticed too!"

"Every guy in town notices, and she seems to enjoy the attention. She likes living on the edge. And Detective Devine is very aware of how Bates is always on the prowl. I wonder how Dan and Lilly became acquainted?"

"Devine left nothing to the imagination. Stop or there will be hell to pay between us, even if you are the chief. It seems Bates made the point that Devine's wife came on to him. That's when they almost came to blows. There was fire in both their eyes, but no fists were in thrown. Bates is somewhat bigger than Devine, but Devine knows how to handle himself. Neither one wanted to let others know what was going on, especially the higher-ups in town government. They didn't know my brother was in another area and witnessed what was going on."

"I think your brother should keep his mouth shut."

"You and I are the only others who know about this. I won't say a word, it's better for everyone, including us."

"But I knew."

"Johnny, it's time to close up. Players are leaving, so let's start cleaning up."

"All right, I'll get to it. I hate sweeping all that shit on the floor. These guys are pigs, but before I start, I need to use the outhouse. Why did you put it so far into the woods?"

"You know why, it stinks like hell."

"It's darker than hell out there, why not put up some lights?"

"Can't do that, remember the neighbors!"

"On top of it all, it's raining like hell. There is mud everywhere."

"Just run between the raindrops."

"Yeah, you try it."

As I was going out the door, I said, *"Jimmy, oh, look who's here. It's Chief Bates."*

"You're early, it's only Sunday night."

"I've something I need to attend to on Monday afternoon. Need a little extra this week, Jimmy."

"Chief, this is getting to be a regular thing."

"You're making more every week, so don't cry to me. I can close you down in a minute, and you know that."

"Then why not do it?"

CHAPTER 5

Surprise

"Look who is here to visit us, and it's still before Saturday noon."

"Jimmy, together they look like something out of a comic movie."

"Johnny, don't ever say that to them, they wouldn't appreciate it."

"I know, I'm just saying that to you. Sal is all of 130 pounds, at five-foot-three, and Dolf is still about 350, and six-foot-five. You know how much I appreciate both of them. It's just that they look different standing side by side."

Salvatore was a slight built man, small pointed face, thin lips, but his hair, always clean, was never held in check and was all over his face usually, like it never saw a comb. He said I need to take a bath every day so I will feel clean and smell clean.

Years ago, he was the headman at the civil engineering department for the state of New Jersey. He hated his job because of all of the politics, every day, all the time, as he put it. So much so that he had a nervous breakdown and retired early to live with his brothers. He was a math whiz who loved to play the ponies using his math skill to pick winners, he believed.

"What brings you two here?"

"Is that young guy Giovanni?"

"Yeah, that's me, Dolf, havent seen you since Jimmy's leaving and the North Africa party."

"You have grown, are you six feet?"

"No, but close to it."

"How much do you weigh?"

"Not close to your weight, about 180."

You're a big youngster, and you look strong."

"Gotta stay in shape. Jimmy says he feels this place won't last very long, and he is thinking of starting a small construction company. Maybe he will hire me."

"Do you play sports?"

"I love baseball."

"Good, I don't understand the game, but it looks like fun."

"Sal, how are all of my great-uncles doing?"

"We are fine, John. Every time I see you, I remember my sister, your grandmother, saying about you, 'That Johnny, he has a nice rounda head.'"

"I remember that, Sal, never knew how to take it. She didn't know how to say handsome, so it's a complement."

"Oh, good. But your head is kinda round. Just grow your hair long, the girls will love it."

"Jimmy, Sal and I are here to talk some business. Should Giovanni leave?"

"Dolf, he knows everything that is going on here, and he understands how to keep things to himself."

"Dolf and Sal, I know how to put my two fingers to my lips and ssh."

"Sally, it's just an old Sicilian way of saying it never happened."

"Well Jimmy, guess who came to see the three of us, me, Carlo, and Charlie yesterday."

"I think I can guess. Am I right? It was the chief."

"Bingo. He has been doing some checking, investigating as he puts it, and knows that we own this old shack, that the electric bills are mailed to our home. He does not know that you give us the dough to pay the bills."

"So what does he want?"

"He wants a kickback, just like I was paying him during my bootleg days. In fact, he continues to arrive at Mary's store every so often, but my

25

paying the bastard is over. He is a cheap creep. Always on the take but no longer from me."

"Don't pay him a dime. Act like you have no idea what is happening up here. I'll take care of him from this end."

"I told him years ago that he needed to watch his back. Ya know years ago while bootlegging, I told him there are other ways to improve our position with him and doing so while we are elsewhere."

"No, none of that. It'll only make the problem bigger. Anyway, soon I will be making a decision about building a small cape and put it up for sale. I've helped Nate, our local bookie, out of a jam, nothing serious, and he said he would lend me the dough to build the spec house I'm considering, interest-free."

"I do not feel this situation can go on much longer. I hear some of the locals complaining that their families are catching on as to why they are short of cash. And those stories in the local paper. It's been good so far, but who knows where it goes. You two stay well, I'll take care of things from here."

CHAPTER 6

You're a Beauty

"When do you expect he will be calling?"

"You encouraged him to take that junket to Frisco, and that's a three-hour time difference, so Danny will probably be at dinner right now. He knows that I usually finish grocery shopping by eight thirty or nine. He'll call in about an hour, say nine thirty."

"That is nice, Lilly, we can play for a while longer."

"Is this what you call playin, Oscar? It's much better than work, but it does take some physical effort. You know how I appreciate that you are a big man."

"Are you talking about my height?"

"You know what I'm talking about."

"How does Danny compare?"

"He's okay. Only okay!"

"How will you keep our friendship from him?"

"When he gets home tomorrow, I'll give him some of this so he'll believe I missed him."

"Do you think that will work?"

"Depends on how well I act."

"God, we are not married, but I hate thinking of you in bed with Danny".

"Oscar, I realize your wife has been gone for almost twenty years, and you have a reputation, you know what I mean."

"And so do you, Lily. You're only thirty-five, you look like twenty-five, blond, blue-eyed, nice ass, and your tits are nice and firm. You are as willing as anyone I've ever met. Do you like kissing them?"

"What do you think?"

"Have you always been that way?"

"In high school and college, I had lots of boyfriends. We had to use the back seat of cars or a nice big couch if I could sneak the guy in when I babysat. But, Oscar, you know I just love sex, bluntly to get laid, and Danny is not enough for me. You just fit in perfectly. Oscar, the other day, while I was picking up some things at the selectmen's office, I noticed you talking to that cute dark-haired, well-built secretary. Are you trying to get friendly with her too? I know you didn't see me, but why were you there?"

"I was meeting with the two most important selectmen."

"Why?"

"As to that young secretary, I was just passing the time."

"Hope so."

"Lilly, it's a long story, has to do with some police work that I can't talk about. Do they have any indication that you and I are seeing one another?"

"Danny is your chief detective—you know what I mean."

"Of course. It's something else completely."

"You have been chief here for quite a while. I'm sure those selectmen and selectwomen are aware of your reputation. Don't let it, your reputation, spoil things."

"It will not, I'm sure. I have some things about most of them that they would not want to see get out, and I know how to quietly use it."

"Oscar, I have another concern about the two new selectwomen. I've been told they are as proper and old-fashioned as my mom was. I'll try to dig something up about them. I think that is going to be very difficult. They were elected as new member to clean things up. Be careful."

"Lilly, you're a beautiful, sexy woman. You know how much I love making love to you, and I don't want Danny to know what is going on. It's almost nine. You must get back to catch that phone call. Let me know

how your sack time with you hubby goes. I want to know if I'm as good in the sack as he is."

"Well, he ain't bad. Variety is the spice of life. And, Oscar, you are a beauty."

"So are you, Lilly."

CHAPTER 7

Lilly's Call

"CHIEF, THERE IS a woman on your private line who is asking to talk with you."

"Did she give you her name?"

"She said it was Lillian, no last name."

"I don't know any Lillian. Anyway, Ruth, put her on and close my door."

"Good morning, is this Lillian? May I have your last name?"

"Oscar, it's me, Lilly."

"I asked you never to call this line."

"Oscar, this is important, I'm pregnant."

"What! Did you tell Danny?"

"No, I'm going to tell him when he gets home tonight. The worst part is I don't know if it is his or yours.

"Holy shit."

"Remember we were together while Danny was in San Francisco, and when he came home that very Saturday afternoon, we made love. And I purposely, as I told you, gave him the best piece of ass he has had in many a day. I did enjoy it too. I hope it's his."

"Do you want to keep the baby?"

"Oscar, I enjoy getting it on with you, but Danny and I have been trying to get pregnant for a couple of years now. I want a baby, and so does he. So what you are suggesting is not going to happen."

"But what if it looks like me? And it's a boy. If it's a blond girl, the situation will be contained."

"Oscar, and our relationship is over for now, but I will keep you informed."

"Do that, and as soon as you can, find out its sex."

"Somehow, we must keep this under wraps. More money may help. Maybe be you can get more from that game in the tar paper shack."

"If I push too hard, they will just close it down. To make matters worse, those two new selectwomen are looking under every rock to discover any wrongdoing to show voters they mean business about cleaning things up. That little article in the town paper sure didn't help. Lilly, stay in touch."

"I will."

"Ruth, I don't know how that Lillian person—she would not give me her last name—how did she get my private number? Please call the telephone company and have that number changed. I hate calls like that."

"Will do, Chief."

"Today! Going out for a while, probably most of the day, Ruth. Need to talk with a few locals. I'll be here early tomorrow morning, probably before you are."

* * *

"Carlo, Charlie, and Sal, I need to come to an understanding with you all. The shack up in the woods that you three own is starting to become a concern around town. I need some hush money to keep it quiet if you all and Jimmy want to keep it going. Judging by the complaints I hear about married men losing their pay, it is sure something has to give. Talk together, all four of you, let us all see what can be done. I bet Dolf will have some ideas. He knows how the game is played."

Oscar seemed to be talking to himself as he left. "What do you think, Sal and Charlie?"

"*Well, Carlo, something is giving him unforeseen concerns. We must think on this. It's not something I want to consider, but it may require more drastic action. But let's hold off, no drastic actions may be necessary. We need more information before considering any future direction.*"

"Sally, all this was going on while as a teen, I was witnessing firsthand the other side of life in a little town north of Boston. There are some things you can't learn in books, especially when what's happening is not on the up-and-up. I just kept my eyes and ears open, not knowing what would happen next."

CHAPTER 8

Pause

"Jimmy, the chief is here."

"What the hell does he want? Johnny, unlock the door, let the scumbag in."

"Jim, we need to talk. Thinks are getting hot, especially with those two old bats on the board."

"Yeah, I heard they on some sort of crusade."

"You can say that again. They want me to appear before the town board of selectmen."

"I got a feeling I know why, Bates. The newspaper article."

"Yeah, that's it. Right on the front page, a picture of a group of women complaining that their husbands are losing their pay at some game that is taking place somewhere in town."

"I have a suggestion, Bates."

"And what's that?"

"We are in late fall, getting colder by the hour. That wood stove in the corner helps some but not enough, so as of this weekend, this place is shut down until it warms up in April or May. No more sharing of profits, 'cause there are none."

"I expected that. I noticed that you applied for a permit to build a new house. From the plans, I saw it looks like a cape."

"How did you know that?"

"You would be surprised how much I know about what goes on in this town."

"Bates, nothing about you surprises me."

"Where did you get the dough to build?"

"That's my business and none of yours."

"Just asking."

"Who is that kid in the corner?"

"He's part of my family, my brother Bill's kid, John. He's here cleaning up, nothing more."

"Big boy, good-looking too."

"Bates—"

"Wait, why don't you call me chief? That's my title."

"You don't deserve to be called anything but Bates. Anyone who has been in this town long enough knows your reputation. Stay away from anyone in our, my, family. I hope you get the message."

"Jimmy, you Sicilians are all alike."

"Maybe in some respects, we are."

"Let me tell you just a little history about Sicilians. Sicily, and the larger cities there, are older than Rome by centuries. Because of its location right in the middle of the Mediterranean Sea, and for that reason, it has become over the centuries a major melting pot of many ethnic people, Greeks, Romans, Jews, Arabs, French, and Spanish, and Normans. Probably many more too. Around AD 1000, it was the most advanced part of the known world."

"So what are you getting to?"

"Sicilians have learned how to live and let live, even if they were taken over by others, which frequently happened. We Sicilians realize we have our faults, but do not try and change us. Why? Because of our long history and all we have endured over the centuries, we believe we are perfect as we are. And that especially applies to our concern and love for our families. Do you understand where I'm coming from?"

"Don't screw with Sicilians."

"You got it, Bates."

"While this was going on, Chief Bates was glancing toward me as if he wanted to say something. I just looked away trying to not look like I knew what they were talking about. Jimmy or even Bates

34

didn't know that I was just starting to become interested in girls and was dating his secretary, Ruth's, daughter, Ellen. She was two years older than I was, good-looking, and being big for my age, we fit pretty well together as a young teen couple. At times, I just wondered what her mom confided in her and how much she knew about town affairs. Working here part-time gave me insights not available to one so young. Maybe I'm just in too far so early in life? But boy, in some ways, it sure was like watching a movie unfold while trying to understand the players and their motives."

CHAPTER 9

Ellen

"*Ellen, here we are, I can't legally drive.*"

"*It's your mom's car, and we're making out every time we are together. I feel like I'm taking advantage of you, or you taking advantage of me?*"

"*You're smart, attractive, love your curly dark hair, just the smell of your body drives me nuts. I like to think of myself as a stud, having the time of my young life. But at the same time, believe it or not, I have, for whatever reason, a belief, the need, not a responsibility just yet, to look after my family, my heritage. I seem to look at everything from my immigrant prospective part of town, where I grew up.*"

"*John Boy, I love that way of saying your name. Your upbringing is just why I'm attracted to you. You just say it like it is.*"

"*Oh, you're putting me on. That Boy part, for me, is getting old.*"

"*I know, but just let's use it for a while?*"

Just between you and me. If you like it, I can live with that. Ellen, why does God put beautiful, hot young girls on earth to tempt young guys like me? I have a difficult time keeping my hands away."

"*I feel the same about you.*"

"*Let's be careful, don't want to become a dad at my age. Ellen, I can tell you things and know that it will never leave this, I was going to say room, but car.*

"*John, and just how fast we got to that point of trust.*"

"I know. That is why I tell you so much about my family, like Dolf and Jimmy and Club Morocco."

"Love your family stories."

"There is much more, but later. What does your mom know about me?"

"Not much, I don't tell her things that we talk about, but I know she likes you."

"Well, at least that's going in the right direction."

"What does she think of the chief?"

"I really don't want to talk about that."

"Why?"

"My mom, Ruth, is forty-five, my dad is gone, and she looks much younger, and Bates is always just a little too friendly. When I'm there to see Mom, she is so protective of me. For me, he gives me the creeps."

"Same for me. The last time I saw him, it was early December, at the club. I had the strangest, almost a concern, for my safety."

"John Boy, that is just how I feel. You know my mom became the chief's secretary after my dad's ship went down in the Pacific, with all the crew lost. He was the captain, and his ship was in a battle with a Jap carrier. The selectmen have helped her, and without her prying, she is privy to lots that goes on in this town."

"Your mom is a redhead—"

"I know, but my dad had straight black hair."

"You could pass for a sweet Sicilian."

"Is that why you are after me?"

"Could be, but you are the whole package, Sicilian or not. Did you see the article about guys losing their pay in a shack in the woods?"

"Yes, I saw that. My mom brought it to my attention 'cause she said that the chief and the selectmen are going to have a meeting about that. But now it seems to have died down."

"That's because the club has been closed for almost three months, nothing is happening."

"So what are you doing? You always seem to have a few dollars to spend."

"When I was cleaning at the club, I did earn a few bucks, enough for a young kid. Now that I'm buying you shakes and burgers, I may have to look for a part-time job."

"Didn't you say you were helping to build that new house with your uncle?"

"Yes, but the weather has closed in, and now that's iffy. Remember it's now New England in January. You know that the club will open again in April or May. I'm not asking you or your mom to do things they are not comfortable with, but if any news is interesting, I would sure like to know about it."

"I do know that the chief is receiving calls so often from a woman named Lillian that he asked my mom to change his private line number two or three times. She said that has never happened before."

"Ellen, let's stop with this stuff about the chief. The older I get, the more I need you close to me. I need a kiss."

"Me too, John Boy."

"I'm not a little boy anymore, Ellen. Careful."

CHAPTER 10

Lilly Again

"Lilly, I'm here at my office but how did you get my number."

"Ruth must have given it to Dan. I just looked in his stuff and found it. Stop changing it. I need to talk with you."

"What is so urgent?"

"I went to my doctor's, and now that I'm five months along, he's not sure, but he believes I'm carrying a boy."

"Oh boy."

"And it is a big baby."

"You still feel the same way."

"I told you I will not have an abortion."

"If this baby looks like you, we all four, you, me, Dan, and the baby, have a big problem. Dan and I have about the same complexion, he is close to my height—"

"Wait, wait, Oscar, Dan looks nothing like you, and if it is a boy, as he grows, the situation will look even worse."

"If it is mine."

"Dan will divorce me for sure. And I will be looking to you for help. Will you pay for that night we both had five months ago or will you leave me to manage on my own? Oscar, I can make it difficult for you. It's not what I want, you know that."

"Lilly, I do realize all that you say. Let me think on it."

"I can't talk any longer. Friday night is my usual grocery shopping night. It's cold and wet this time of year, and I'm tired and getting bigger by the day."

"Be careful, Lilly, you may be carrying my baby. I just heard a noise from another part of the station. Oh, down the hall, it's the cleaning guy talking with the night officer. I forgot he is usually here by this time, after regular station hours for the public. Do you always shop on Friday night? Why?"

"Because the markets start to quiet down, and I like it better that way. I'm usually home before nine—it works for me and Dan."

"I have a meeting scheduled with the selectman's office next Friday afternoon, but I should be here by six or so. Call me about this time so we can talk again about our situation."

"I will. Oscar, don't let that meeting drag on. We must come to some agreement about our, I said our, problem."

"Lilly, I can't change the time. The selectmen are important to my position as chief in this town, so if I'm not here, it's because they are the long-winded ones."

"Is it about the gambling story that was in the papers a while back?"

"I think so, but things seem to have quieted down."

"Hope so, we'll see. Let's talk next week."

CHAPTER 11

The Day After

"Hı, Jᴀᴋᴇ, ʜᴏᴡ *are things with you? Want some morning coffee?"*

"Nah, I'm good. My job at the supermarket is just about holding things together. I'm just wondering if you plan to open the shack when the weather warms. I know lots of guys still enjoy a game on the weekends, and I can use the money as a table man, but only on weekends."

"Did you see the articles in the paper?"

"Yes, I did, that's why I'm asking. I also see you are building a new house. Will that get in the way of the games?"

"It depends, Jake, things are kind of touchy right now, but in a few months, I will be able to give a better answer."

"You know, my wife's sister works at the police station."

"Who is your wife's sister?"

"Ruth Smith, the chief's assistant. No kidding. Jim, last night, she told my wife that yesterday, the chief was grilled by the selectmen, especially the two old broads new to the board about gambling somewhere in town, and they want progress made to correct the situation."

"The local paper is about to cover the meeting for the next issue. Jake, we need time to for this to cool down."

"Ruth told my wife that with the town elections coming up in March, these two selectwomen may find competition for their seats. They

are ruffling too many feathers in town. Interesting to see how the vote goes at town meeting time."

"Does your wife's sister have any other interesting information?"

"All she says is that the chief seems to have something going on with someone named Lillian, no last name. Jim, everyone knows the chief's reputation. Speaking of Ruth, there she is. Ruth, what are you doing here?"

"After what I just found out, I need a good cup of strong coffee this morning. Maybe something stronger."

"What is going on?"

"Dan Devine's wife, Lilly, was involved in a terrible accident when driving home from grocery shopping last night. The roads were all snow and ice—she slid off the road down an embankment and hit a tree dead center. All she said was, 'Police, police,' and went unconscious. And she is more than five months pregnant. She must have been down against the tree for a while. If not for her headlights being on, it could have been all night. That Chestnut Hill is bad in the winter. The officer at the scene said someone was on the wrong side of the road, and it was not Lilly, and whoever it was drove off without stopping. Dan is with her right now. Lilly and the unborn baby are in very serious condition. I expect that Dan will be out for a while, but I'm sure he will be available after talking with the emergency room doctors and the specialist who have been with her."

"What is the condition of the baby?"

"Too early to tell just yet."

CHAPTER 12

What If

"DOLF, YOU HAVE more experience than the three of us dealing with Oscar. Something is fishy. He struts himself around town as if he is God's gift to the place including every woman he comes in contact with. Jimmy tells me that some women named Lillian has been calling him at his office on a somewhat regular schedule, at night when few people are around. I've been told that the calls have stopped. Does that seem odd?"

"Who told you that?"

"Jim said that Bates's assistant, his secretary, Ruth, knows lots of stuff, mostly keeps it to herself, but even for her, it's getting to be too much to handle."

"My nephew John is dating Ruth's daughter. Every once in a while, she tells him something interesting."

"What do you think, Sal? You're the college guy and smarter than all of us together. I think it is odd that Devine's wife has a name that sounds like Lillian, that person who was calling Bates. Is Lilly short for Lillian? Could it be that they are one and the same person? Just speculation on my part. Was something going on between Lilly and Bates? Long and short of it, just thinking out loud."

"We are starting to sound like that detective Sherlock Holmes. Let's not get ahead of ourselves, boys. Charlie, you're not saying much."

"Well, Carlo, I would not put anything past Bates?"

"He was by here a few days after Lilly Devine's car crash."

"Why, Sal?"

"He is putting pressure on us because Carl didn't get a building permit for that barn he's building out back. I told him that is a concern for the building department, not him. Always looking for something, you know what I mean. We got into a hot argument. He even pushed me up against the wall. He's a hell of a lot bigger than me. Wanted to swing at him, but I would get the worst of it. His words, 'You fucking Sicilians are all alike, I don't trust you, and I will never turn my back on anyone of you.' I told him I felt the same way about him. He left swearing all the way to his fancy police car."

"Dolf, did you talk with Jimmy about reopening the shack?"

"I did. He's just trying to see how hot the news is regarding gambling in town and also knows that if the chief comes around for his take, the coast will be clear for reopening, maybe late April or early May, when it's warmer."

"Sal, what's your take on the election? It looks to me that both, or at least one, of the new women selectmen will not make it. Their offending everyone with all their bullshit probing into every little part of town government. One thing about Bates, he has been chief for almost twenty-five years and has something on so many people that he is dangerous. Lots of enemies. I'll bet he has something on each of those women or members of their families. If not in writing but in his head, and he'll use it when necessary."

"Jimmy tells me that after the election, in early April, he will get the shack in order, make sure the equipment is okay, find out if the table guys want in again, and get Johnny to help on weekends. Jim said he is now bigger, stronger, handsome, and is a good worker. The girls like him too. His girlfriend Ellen may provide some news so he, John, will be able to give us just a little information. Then he'll know where it stands about opening. That was Jim's take. Let's get together after the election."

"Sounds good."

CHAPTER 13

Election Results

"ONE OF THE women on the board of selectmen was returned to office."

"Which one?"

"Martha Tines."

"How do you know that so soon, Jimmy?"

"John Boy heard that from his girlfriend, Ellen, Ruth's daughter. Ruth works election results and has done that for years and knows before results are announced and in the paper."

"Jimmy, don't call him John Boy. He's no longer a boy but a good-looking young man."

"I know, Dolf, can't help it. I've known him all his life."

"I always use Giovanni, he seems to like it."

"Well, I have more to bring you four up-to-date about our police department, and Bates in particular. And it comes indirectly from Ruth, via Ellen and Giovanni. It seems that Bates received a visit from Martha Tines before the election. Ruth overheard a somewhat heated conversation. They were trying to keep it down, but both let it get out of hand. Tines started to push Bates. Here is how it went down."

"Hold on, Mrs. Tines. Let me bring you up-to-date about what I know. Your attorney husband likes to play the ponies. He fashions himself as someone who knows horses because he grew up on a farm up country. You have, because of your old family wealth, bailed him out on a num-

ber of occasions. He usually has a substantial amount due with the local bookie, Nate. Am I correct about that? In addition, you know very well where the card games take place. Your husband, the attorney, has been there quite often. He usually comes up short there too."

"That's when Tines left in a huff"

"She is no longer in a strong position. Maybe that is good for the games to go on."

"You may be right, Sal. Too early to tell."

"A short time later, Dan Devine arrived for a scheduled appointment with Bates. According to Ruth, it went something like this."

"Chief, what the hell is going on about the accident that has put my wife's life in danger and that of the baby she is carrying?"

"First, Dan, is she making any progress? What does she remember?"

"She is not conscious, Bates, and all she ever says is, 'Police, police.' She has a scar on the side of her head where she must have slammed against the steering wheel when she hit the tree. It's beneath her hair, so it won't show. She may, according to the doctors, not ever remember what happened that night. If she dies, the baby dies. Look, Chief, one of the officers on duty that night said that it looked to him that as she came around the corner, someone forced her off the road, left, and made no effort to help. Thank God another driver noticed her lights on. But that was long after the accident took place. Bates, what the hell are you doing to investigate what happened, or do I have to get involved?"

"You know you can't. Lilly is family, and policy prohibits your involvement. We're working on it, but I must say, it's an almost impossible case to solve. No witnesses, all traces of clues melting away."

"Devine also left in a huff, mad as hell."

"Any ideas, Jimmy?"

"Yeah. One, Dan is a damn good police detective, and he is not one to just sit there and wait for things to develop. He may be a smooth-speaking voice and have been told he could have been a radio announcer if he wanted to but loves police work. When he gets his teeth into a case, he will not let go. He is about forty years old, been married to Lilly for more than ten years, and he loves his beautiful wife's long legs, his description. They are considered to be the most attractive couple in town. He is very possessive of her, especially when other men show an interest, no matter who."

"Carlo, seems that you and Sal had a run-in with the chief a while ago."

"As usual, he was looking for a cut, for what I don't know. He does know that we three own the building for your games. That's why he is putting a touch on you. I understand he pushed Sal."

"He did, left swearing and saying things about our heritage. That just does not sit well will with all of us."

"I know."

"We're almost into April. It will start to warm up, and maybe we can get just one more profitable summer of games in. I know this will not last forever, but if you agree that I can use the shack, I will slowly start cleaning things up."

"Okay, okay."

CHAPTER 14

The Situation

"I KNEW THE four of you would be here having breakfast."

"We meet here at least two times a week just to chew the fat."

"Well, I have some fat for you all to chew on and need your ideas."

"Here is what happened two days ago. I've started to clean Club Morocco."

"What did you call that shack?"

"Oh, that's a name that Giovanni and I call the place. It's a long story—no, I will not go into it now. We, John and I, were getting the place ready for later when it warms up some. I even found some dry firewood for the stove to get rid of the chill and left him there alone. I had to leave and take care of a situation with the cape house I'm building and told him I expected to be open again by the end of April or early May. Be gone for a couple hours, I said. After about a half hour, Bates showed up looking for me and said he would wait until I returned. He told Bates it would be a while. All of a sudden, he felt someone right behind and then a hand on his ass, and another from behind grabbing his balls and pecker."

"What!"

"Wait, there is more. John jumped away and said to Bates, 'I've been told to be careful around you but figured it was just with girls and women. You're a fuckin' pervert.' He looked at Bates, in his red eyes—

they looked like it was the devil, Satan from hell, he said, looking at him. 'But John,' Bates said, 'we could have lots of fun together, and I can take care of your money needs. You don't make much here. It's your uncle, he's the money man, not you. Think about it!' With that, John just walked out back behind the outhouse into the woods, swearing as he left. Then Bates said, 'You ginnies, you dagos, are all alike, young or old.' John said to me, growing up in an immigrant neighborhood, with people from many countries, he knew that all of them were better than Bates. He said, 'I wanted to spit in his face.' He waited over a day before he told me what happened. Bates was gone when I got back. I got hold of myself, remembered the well in Sicily in 1943. You all know that story."

"We do, but it's a two-fingers-to-the-lips story."

"I remembered the well way back on your land."

"Wait, Jimmy," all three chimed in, too close, too much to risk.

"Dolf, from your bootleggin' days, you must have connections, in Boston or even Providence."

"I still know people, but what are you suggesting?"

"I don't know, but I need some advice."

Then Charlie, who usually is quiet, said, *"Dolf, why not ask a connected friend how we could solve this situation so that it could be considered a mob hit job. No one likes the bastard anyway, and the number of suspects would be quite large."*

"Including us," Carlo said.

"Charlie worked as a machinist by trade. Always came up with well-considered ideas before he spoke. Just a little, kinda round man who would take yearly vacations to Italy, writing back with detailed descriptions of the places he visited, and always with a pride for his and our ancestry. He was another of my light-skinned Sicilian relatives who looked delicate, but his eyes always looked like they were hiding something."

Charlie went on, *"This situation and what we all seem to be considering is dangerous for everyone concerned. We do not want to overreact. But this cannot continue. That, I believe, is where we are all, at least in our minds."*

"I realize that, but let's make sure of what we plan and all have the same story, and as always, fingers to the mouth."

"Right, right, Dolf. Let me talk with some friends down south, then meet again and see where we are."

"We all feel this way. Never, never go after and cause pain to the wife or children of a Sicilian's family. And this is the worst type of pain! That is exactly what took place here."

"Agreed?"

"Agreed! This will take some time and necessary planning no matter what we do or not do."

"How is John reacting to what happened?"

"Just keeps it to himself, not a word."

CHAPTER 15

A Visitor

"*WELL, HELLO, UNCLE Salvatore, what brings you to the club?*"

"*I see you practicing your swing, so I wanted to ask you a few questions about baseball.*"

"*I didn't think you ever took an interest in my sports games.*"

"*You're right, usually. But yesterday, just by chance, I turned on the radio and listened to a little of the first game of the year between the Red Sox and another team, I think it was from New York.*"

"*Oh, that was the Yankees.*"

"*Yes, that's it. It was played in Boston at a place called Fenway.*"

"*Fenway Park, that's where they play half of their games each year.*"

"*I heard the announcer say that this tall guy, Ted—*"

"*That's Ted Williams, their best player.*"

"*That's the one. He hit the ball about four hundred feet for a home run. The announcer said, 'Boy can Ted swing that stick.' What does he mean, the stick?*"

"*That's a bat, like the one you see me here sometimes as I try to improve my swing.*"

"*I'm starting to enjoy the game. You know I was an engineer when I was younger, and it seems to me that this man Ted approaches his bat swings like it was a science.*"

"*That is just how he approaches it, Uncle Sal.*"

"Can I see your bat?"

"Sure, but I don't have it here now. I'll bring it here tomorrow and show it to you."

"You don't suppose that swinging a bat is the same motion as chopping wood or, I hate to say this, but beheading a chicken."

"Nah, nothing like it. I know 'cause I saw my grandmother, Ma, your sister, butcher chickens."

"Ever see them run around without their head?"

"Yeah, blood everywhere."

"Jimmy told me what happened a while back with chief Bates."

"Ah, damn, I wish he didn't do that. I can take care of myself."

"John, he is a dangerous grande strunz."

"I know, Uncle. Remember, until I was five, I could speak lots of Sicilian Italian. Lost most of it when I started school, but I remember lots. What does it mean?"

"It means a big shit. A dangerous big shit. Remember that."

"Don't worry, I will."

"What are you up to today? Jimmy must have told you that it looks like he will open Club Morocco by about May the first. You like that name."

"I do. I suggested it, but we don't advertise to attract attention. It's only by word of mouth that we attract players."

"I bet the chief knows what's going on. Still likes his cut. I'll bet he is good for five hundred a week at times when things really get going. Has he been around?"

"No, not yet."

"Giovanni, keep the place warm, be careful. Must get back to my brothers, and maybe I'll see Dolf. Since his stroke years ago, he has slowed some."

"I know, but strong as an ox, still."

CHAPTER 16

Remembering

"Dan, you have a call."

"Ruth, do I have to now?"

"It's the nurse who is assigned to Lilly."

"I'll be right there."

"Lilly is starting to awaken. Keeps yelling something, 'Gotta go.' She kept screaming 'big black police car' over and over, did that for about ten minutes. That is when I called you. Now she is as quiet as before. That happens sometimes with coma patients. You can sit here for a while if you want. Let me ask you a few questions."

"Sure, what's on your mind?"

"First, she seems healthy except for losing a few pounds."

"Is that a good sign?"

"I'm not her doctor, but when she comes out of her coma, she should be fine. May not remember about the accident but that is normal, I think."

"How will the baby do through all of this?"

"Make an appointment with her doctors. They will give you better answers than I can. Detective Devine, I feel that your wife is starting to come around. Let's pray for the baby."

"Ruth, is anyone looking for me?"

"No, except the chief wanted to know where you went. I told him the hospital. How is Lilly doing? I hope better."

"I need to meet with her doctors about her and the baby she is carrying. Oscar, there you are."

"I heard you and Ruth. Looks like the situation is improving."

"I hope so. I have some business to attend to so I'm off. Ruth, do you have the duty roster the night of Lilly's accident?"

"Easy to find."

"Let me have it."

"He comes on duty at five p.m. Yes, that's right. It was Ross."

"Do you have his home number?"

"Tom, It's Dan Devine. Sorry to bother you at night, but do you remember the night of Lilly's accident?"

"Yeah, I was on duty that night."

"The record for that night indicates that only three people were at the station. You, the cleaning man Al, and the chief."

"Sounds right."

"When did you see either of them, and when did they leave?"

"I'm doing this from memory, so I could be off, but here is my recollection. If the chief works late, it is usually about six p.m. that he would arrive."

"When did he leave?"

"About nine p.m."

"Did you see him between those hours?"

"No, but he is at the other side of the building, and I had no reason to visit with him."

"Keep this talk to yourself."

"I will for sure."

"Al, this is Dan Devine, from the police."

"I know your voice, Dan, why are you calling?"

"I need to ask for some information on the q.t."

"Police work?"

"You can call it that. Let's keep this talk quiet."

"Okay, if that is what you want."

"The night of my wife's auto accident, you were cleaning the station."

"Yes, I was, and it was a mess because of the snow, sleet, and rain."

"What time did you arrive?"

"It could have been about five thirty."

"When did you leave?"

"I usually do the job in one hour, but this time I was there until seven fifteen or so."

"Did you see anyone?"

"I did see Tom Ross, who had night duty."

"Anyone else?"

"No… Wait, a little after seven, I saw the chief as he came out of the bathroom, just after I cleaned it. That was my last area to clean, and I left."

"Thanks, Al. Remember, quiet about this talk."

"Ruth, does anyone ever use the rear entrance?"

"Not that I know of, but only you, the chief, and maybe the senior sergeant have keys, and I'm not sure of the sergeant."

"Just working on something. Is the chief in?"

"I'm right here, Dan, let's go into my office. You're on to something, Dan. What's going on?"

"Oscar, you know me. When I get my teeth into a case, I will be pushy and blunt until I'm satisfied that I have the story straight. I think you're the bastard that drove Lilly off the road and caused the accident."

"What the hell, are you nuts! What are you accusing me of?"

"You had plenty of time to leave this place, drive up to Chesterfield Hill, and force her off the road."

"You're out of your mind. Why the hell would I do that? What is my motive? You're the detective, tell me."

"Did you have something going on with my wife? Why the hell are you sending me on junkets all over the country?"

"You know why, Dan. You will probably be chief one day, and I want the best qualified person to head this police department. Now I'm not sure it's you."

"Do you know what Lilly is screaming at the hospital, over and over? BIG BLACK POLICE CAR. Our police cars are two shades of green, and not black. Yours is the only black car. When and if Lilly recovers, I will have a sure answer, and she is slowly getting better. If I'm right, Chief, the shit is going to hit the fan, and maybe sooner than one can guess. Do you know how the people of this town refer to you? One of two ways, the ass man or the professor of love."

CHAPTER 17

Unexpected Visitor

"Uncle Jim, a police officer is walking toward us."

"Unlock the door and let him in. Hi, Dan, what's up?"

"You must know, Jim, that the force knows what takes place here, usually on the weekends."

"Dan, it's hard to keep secrets in a small town, and these are just a bunch of guys playing cards and blowing off a little steam, having a few beers."

"But you do know that the pressure is on by some in this town to close this down."

"Ya know, there are games like this going on in rich and poor homes all the time. This place is just off the beaten path and not harming any-one. I don't force the guys to come here, purely their choice."

"I get it, but just the same, this is not going to last."

"That is why I'm starting to build homes to make a few bucks.

"I'm not here about closing you down. I will keep my reasons to myself and want you to forget I was here today."

"Get right to it."

"Does Chief Bates ever show up here?"

"Mostly on a Monday afternoon, but at times late in the evening when we are about to shut down."

"What happens when he is here?"

"Dan, you've been around. Do I need to spell it out?"

"No, does he come every week?"

"Usually…"

"The story is that you are planning to open again, probably in early May."

"Correct."

"Will Bates show up?"

"He'll be here on Sunday night with his hand out because it will be our first weekend this year."

"Do you mean shaking your hand?"

"Yeah, that too."

"The place is clean, bright inside, looks like hell from outside, but what about a bathroom? With the players smoking and drinking beer all night, they must need to take a piss."

"We set up an old outhouse about twenty-five yards that way in the woods."

"Can I use it?"

"Sure, my nephew, John, will set you in the right direction."

"Who is this kid John?"

"He's my brother's son. I pay him a few dollars to clean up. He says its going toward a college education."

"Can I talk with John?"

"Sure."

"I just want to ask him a few questions."

"Hi, John, I'm Dan Devine."

"Yeah, I know who you are."

"Have you ever had any dealings with the chief?"

"No, why do you ask that question? Uncle Jim, have you said anything to Devine?"

"No."

"Please don't."

"I'm not pushing you, John. I have the answers I want. Jim, do you mind if I take John off to the side? I need to ask him some question that probably only he knows about."

"You okay with that, John?"

"Sure, Uncle Jim."

Sally, I won't get into this meeting, but Devine and I came to an understanding—our willingness to be helpful to one another. That is all I will say, police business."

"Jim, do you own this shack?"

"No, Dan. My great-uncles do, my mom's brothers."

"Where are they?"

"About a half mile down the street."

"Can I talk with them?"

"Not a problem, they're usually home in the morning."

* * *

"There's a cop at our front door."

"I know him, he's the detective on our force. It's Dan."

"Yes, Charlie, it is. Do you mind if I ask the three of you a few questions?"

"Are you on police business?"

"Yes, I know you three own the card game shack up in the woods."

"We do. Is that why you are here?"

"No, other police business. Have either of you had meetings with the chief?"

"You mean Bates."

"Why does he show up here?"

"Sal, you answer that question."

"Bluntly, he has his hand out because he knows we own the shack, and he thinks we get part of the weekends take. We don't get a dime nor do we ask for one, so I refused, for all of us, to pay that bastard a dime. We almost came to blows. He hates us Sicilians. We have no love for him either."

"Sal, he seems to have it in for lots of people. Last question, is that baseball bat for protection?"

"No, but it could be, I guess. It's here because I just want to understand American sports better so I can talk easier with John Boy. He loves baseball, and I want to show him I have an interest too. Starting to like and understand the game a little."

CHAPTER 18

Sound Advice

"THE LAST TIME I saw them, Sal, Carlo, Charlie, and Dolf, they were all at the table enjoying a spaghetti and meatball supper, washing it down with Dolf's homemade red wine. I will always remember the aroma of that place, not just the kitchen, but the entire house. And the Italian cold cuts. God, I wish I was there with them right now. I can just guess their colorful conversation—old times and family responsibilities and the love for one another, family."

"Dolf, did you hear from your friends?"

"Yes, it was simple—go slow, don't overreact, keep your heads about you. If you act in haste, it will be a mistake. There are situations that time and developments can change your opportunities for the better. Another note of concern, they do not like the idea of making it look like a mob hit. It is not big enough for that. Maybe it's better to make it appear to be a local vendetta or robbery. He does have cash on him most times and does have a reputation that goes beyond our town. But he is small potatoes to the boys down south."

"Did you hear that we are having visits from the police, Dan Devine, the chief detective in town? Something is setting him on a path like a bloodhound."

"How is his wife, Lilly, coming along?"

"John's girlfriend says she appears to be coming out of the coma. Keeps yelling something that gives Dan lots of concern."

"Who told you that, Charlie?"

"It was John who picked it up from his girlfriend, via her mother. For a young kid, he knows his way around. And I heard from John that Devine and he had a nice long conversation a few days ago. John would not say what was talked about."

"Devine is up to something. He's digging just a little too deep, even asked me about the baseball bat that is in the front hall. Thinks I'm an old baseball fan or that I'm keeping it for protection. But he is smarter than that. He could help us if he felt comfortable, especially with me. I like the guy as opposed to the SOB chief."

"Do you have something on your mind and with Devine?"

"No, no, just running ideas around my old head."

What do you think, Dolf?"

"Let's put this down for a while. But I just can't stand the SOB."

"We all feel the same."

CHAPTER 19

Awake

"Doctor, I received your message that my wife is awake and is gaining control of her surroundings."

"Just bit by bit, Dan."

"When can I see her?"

"Give us and her some time. It would be better if you visit tomorrow afternoon. Don't worry, she is doing better, and I will tell her of your many visits."

"How is the baby doing?"

"I'm not her maternity physician; however, things are looking better from what he tells me. Be there tomorrow."

* * *

"Lilly, I was here yesterday and just about every day. Let me hug you. It has been long and difficult for you. Thank God you're getting stronger and better."

"How long have I been here?"

"Too long, but we can get more into that as you improve."

"No, I want to know now? I'm pregnant. Is the baby well? What happened?"

"You don't remember?"

"What should I be remembering?"

"Your doctors said things will come back piece by piece, but it could take time. Let's leave all that for another day. I will be here again every day. We can talk more as you gain strength and are able to move about. Right now I have pressing duties at the station. And I can see I'm tiring you."

* * *

"Good morning, Ruth, is the chief in?"

"Hi, Dan. Yes, but he said he is not to be disturbed."

"Well, you tell him it is important, and I will talk with him."

"I just told him and he said give him ten minutes."

"Oscar, I was just in to visit with Lilly. She is no longer comatose, and the docs say she will slowly get her memory back. Now. You know me, I get right to right to the point. The officer who arrived at the accident location first said that Lilly was saying, before she passed out, that it was a big black police car that forced her off the road. My belief is that you are involved in this accident—it could be solved when she recovers her memory. You're the only one who has a black police vehicle in this town."

"Dan, what the hell are you insinuating? You're way off base. This is destroying any good that existed between us. How many big black cars are there in this town? Why the hell would I do something like that to your wife? As far as you taking my position when I retire, that is out of the question. I'll suggest a search for someone outside the department to selectmen."

"So be it, Oscar. But if you are involved in the accident, I will find what your motive is, you can bet on that."

"Dan, be careful. You're not on solid ground."

"Is that a threat, Oscar?"

* * *

"Good afternoon, Mrs. Peterson. I'm Detective Devine."

"I know who you are, Officer Devine. I've seen your picture in the paper."

"You live behind the police station and have a good view from your windows of the comings and goings at the station's rear entrance."

"I do, but I'm not a busy body watching any of you."

"I realize that, but I have a special question. Do you ever see any of our officers using the rear exit, especially at night?"

"It does not appear to be used very often, but when anyone is there late, I do see someone using it."

"And who is that?"

"I'm not sure, but I believe it's Chief Bates. I think he goes out for coffee and then is back to the station."

"Does he return using the rear door?"

"I guess so, but I'm not watching all the time."

"Do you wear glasses?"

"Sometimes, but just for reading."

"Do you know the color of his car?"

"It's a dark color, like blue or maybe black. Oh, sometimes the chief arrives with another car."

"What other car?"

"It's really a pickup truck, that's when he brings his little dog with him. He does have a dog. I think the dog's name is Maxie, a little mutt."

"I didn't know that."

"Officer Devine, he really seems to love that dog."

"How can you tell?"

"Well, he usually leaves water and food for the dog, leaves the truck window open to give it some air, and the dog just sits in the truck, well trained and waits for him to return. Officer Devine, am I involved in some investigation? Should I be concerned?"

"No, no, just let's keep our talk between the two of us. Just regular police business."

CHAPTER 20

Why

"GOOD MORNING, LILLY. *Your doctors tell me that you're feeling much better and seem to be remembering lots more each day."*

"I am, Dan, but there are many fuzzy situations and things that are not just right."

"Like what?"

"I'm starting to recall some things about the night of my accident. I know I was sort of pushed off the road by another big black car that was almost on my side of Chestnut Hill Road. I always come home that way after grocery shopping."

"Do you remember any more about that other car?"

"One of the staff nurses here told me I was screaming 'police, police,' but I can't remember why."

"Lilly, as your husband, not as a police officer, I must ask you about Oscar. Were you involved with him when I was away on police business? It seems you are unresponsive or unwilling to answer my question, why?"

"What are you suggesting, Dan?"

"I am suggesting, but you and I both know his reputation, and I remember just how we became acquainted. You know I love you, Lilly, but how do I say this. Can I trust you when it comes to other men? Have you been fooling around behind my back with Oscar?"

"What makes you say that?"

"I think it was the chief who forced you off the road."

"Why would he do that?"

"Lilly, I'm a damn good detective, and my gut usually leads me in the right direction even if I don't want to go there."

"Dan, you know I have always needed the love of a good man. You know that. Yes, I have been friendly with Oscar, but it's you who I love, and it's you I want to have a family with."

"Just how friendly were you with Oscar?"

"Dan, I don't remember much beyond the accident."

"Lilly, for both of us and for the baby you are carrying, I hope this does not cause us both more grief. If this baby is Oscar's, that's where I'm going with this right now, then we will be headed for a divorce. That's where I draw the line. Do you understand that, Lilly?

"I do. I do. But in my heart, I know it is yours."

"Lilly, I hope you have not been screwing around. If you have, bad things will happen to all involved."

"Dan, I've matured a lot during these last months. I will always love you, please understand that. I'm only human, I do make mistakes."

"I hope you didn't with Oscar."

CHAPTER 21

Why Here

"CHIEF, I DIDN'T expect you until Monday afternoon."

"Jim, now that your reopened, I just wanted to see how things are going."

"As I'm sure you know, not too bad."

"How does the rest of the summer look?"

"It depends on the powers to be and how they like being here again, you know what I mean."

"I do—it depends upon providing what is necessary."

"And what's that? You're putting me on. Here is your take. Maybe as the word gets out, it'll grow a bit."

"I hope so. This stinks, given all that risk is on me."

"Chief, I'm closing up. Even my cleanup kid, my nephew, has gone home. That's where I want to be. It's later than usual—need my beauty sleep. Do you hear a dog barking?"

"That's just Maxie. She's out on my pickup and will quiet down. Just a nice little mutt, no problem. I need a piss, so keep the lights on for a while."

"No can do, Chief. We never use lights. Don't want my distant neighbors to know where it is. Besides, now that the rain has stopped, the light from the full moon is beautiful, lights your way. I'm locking up. You use the outhouse. See you next week."

"Who the hell is in that shithouse?"

"Don't bang on the door, I'm coming out."

"What the hell are you doing here?"

"I knew this was your usual stop before leaving. Been here the last two nights waiting for you, and this is as good a place to get some things off my chest about you. You must be watching your back, Oscar. I've never heard that you carried a gun, a .38 police special, I'm guessing. I can see it there because of the bulge in your jacket. And you're never without that chief badge of yours. Does it help you get your way with women? You go after them, old, young, teens, and married or not. And now, Chief, you're after young boys too. You are a real piece of shit, Oscar. Your reputation is all around town. I'll bet there are ten guys that have it in for you. No wonder the gun."

"Who the hell do you think you are talking to me like that?"

"Just one of many who hates your guts. One other thing, you seem to especially dislike Sicilians. I know that is true, I've heard some of your darning words. Is it all newcomers to the US that you dislike? What about old bootleggers and the guys who run the number in town? Bet they are all paying off too."

"You act like all those you mention are the best of our townspeople. They're not. I'm just keeping things in line."

"And getting paid on the side?"

"Right, and it's worth every cent to keep things peaceful for the rest of the townspeople. What are you looking at behind me? Someone else is here with you?"

"No, don't, don't." The club hit the side of his head with a loud thud. Sounded like an ax on the first swing bringing down a dead tree. Oscar fell on his hands and knees, digging his fingers into the muddy earth, trying to get up. The next three swings finished the job. One to each side of the head and the last right on the top. Blood was everywhere.

"I just wanted you to break both his legs."

"But he started to turn around and must have guessed someone else was here. Had to act fast. I just could not forget all the evil he has inflicted on so many people in this town. I hate the bastard, and

67

it was just something I couldn't control. He earned every knock on his big head. Had it coming for years."

"What is done is done. We must keep our heads about this. First let's make it look like a robbery. Take the dough. No, the front right pocket. See the lump in that pocket? Leave a few bucks on the ground like it was done in a hurry. Let's walk back toward the club about halfway and then into the woods. Less tracks. First cover his body with some cut branches, get rid of the bat deeper into the woods. Wash the mud off your shoes and burn the gloves. Now let's get the hell out of here, fast."

CHAPTER 22

He Turned White

"SALLY, HE TURNED white like he was about to faint."

Devine's words were, *"Oh my god, it's the chief. He's even wearing his badge—his .38 is still where it belongs, in its holster. Has anyone been near the body?"*

"Officer Devine, I saw it first, got my uncle, and ran down to call the station. Uncle Jim and I are the only two who have been near the area."

"Everyone clear the area. Officer, for thirty feet around the chief's body, in a big circle, put out crime tape. Is there a phone in the shack?"

"No, but the closest is at my great-uncle's place down the street."

"Officer, you stay here, no one gets close. I need to make a call to the coroner."

Just then, Maxie, the chief's mutt, ran up to the body and started to whimper. Almost sounded like an infant softly crying.

"And get that dog the hell out of here. Put it in the chief's truck. Maybe that will keep it quiet."

The coroner arrived in the late of the afternoon. *"What time was the body found?"*

"About two hours ago."

"My estimate is that he has been dead for more than about fourteen hours. You can move the body now to my lab, and I will, after further investigation, give the cause of death, but from what I can see, it looks

like blunt force to the head area. I'll provide a written report as soon as possible."

"As the chief's body was being removed, card players were starting to arrive and told the place was closed. That's when the story of the murder of Chief Bates quickly spread. Sally, the next day, the local paper and all the Boston papers, the *Globe*, the *Post* and area papers were all over the story. Pictures were being taken of the shack but they were not allowed to go anywhere near the outhouse. One even titled it the 'Outhouse Murder and Robbery.' It was big news in all of greater Boston papers. The chief's reputation was quietly known through Breakheart. Devine started to round up suspects starting with Uncle Jim, Dolf, the local bookie, Nate, my great-uncles, Carlo, Sal, and Charlie, and even some of the guys who were regular players at Club Morocco. Even Attorney Tines. Lots of suspects, but nothing was pointing to any one particular person or persons. Devine did say to newspapers that it looked as if more than one person was involved but would not give reasons or the names of suspects. Everyone was given the third degree. No one was ultimately considered a prime suspect.

"Sally, from my point of view, I don't believe Dan or any other town officials wanted to find the murderers. Without saying so, they were looking for the chief to retire. This only made for a fast decision as to a replacement. Martha Tines, more vocal than ever, began to push on Dan Devine about the gambling shack in the woods. Devine also knew about Tine's husband's gambling problems and assured her that the situation would be addressed quickly, but he had the murder to deal with first. Two related events took place about a week apart. One, three weeks after the murder, and the second, about ten days later. The selectmen's office appointed Dan Devine as the new chief without a long search, because Devine was second in authority to Bates and it made the transition quicker. Next, the gambling shack in the woods, in a spectacular fire, burned to the ground. Nothing was left, not even the chairs and tables. The fire department suggested that the old wood stove was the cause even if it occurred during the early summer."

CHAPTER 23

My Story

"John Boy—"

"Stop saying that John Boy BS. I'm now in my last year of college, making love to my professor who keeps pumping me for some of my history."

"But bring me up-to-date as to how things turned out for all of your players, the suspects."

"Why, so you can write your book and then leave me high and dry?"

"I wouldn't do that."

"I wonder. Remember I'm still, compared to you, a little green behind the ears, but have seen more than most by now."

"Says you. Come on, I'll give you a reward. How about we share in the profits if I publish and make some big money? What do you say? Put it in writing."

"Here is what I know. Been out of my town, Breakheart, for a while now. Lilly never recovered her memory, or so she says. That is my 'so she says.' Sometime after the fire, she had a healthy baby girl, blond, blue eyes. She and Dan two years later had another child, this time a boy. Then bad, very bad, news. Dan was involved in a high-speed police car chase and was killed in an accident. He ran into a big dump truck, killed instantly. I liked Dan, very much, became a good friend. Lilly is now a widower with two young children, still good-looking, I'm told. Probably looking for another guy, this time with money.

"Three of my four great-uncles are no longer with us. Only Carlo, the youngest, is here today. Except for Carlo, they were in their seventies while the club was operating. Dolf had another stroke, and this time he did not make it. I do miss them all. They were a big part of my heritage. They were my good friends.

"Uncle Jim is in the construction business and doing very well—still does not know how to handle all the dough he makes, but he is happy and married. Still likes to play cards and visit the ponies at Suffolk Downs. When I do see him, he puts two fingers to his mouth. My dad does the same, I guess it's just my family's ways.

"About a year after the shack burned down, I found out that Devine, a week after the murder of Bates, found a baseball bat, a Clyde Vollmer model, in the woods near the outhouse. It was covered with hair and dried blood. He never said a word about it except to me.

"That seems strange. Who was Clyde Vollmer?"

"He was a Red Sox player. Not a big star, although one year, in twenty-one games, hit thirteen home runs, three in one game. I may have had or used one of his bats while in high school. The Williams bat is still in the front hall of Carlo's house. I'll bet the place smells just the same, meatball and red pasta sauce with garlic and mushrooms. Great red wine too.

"Given what Lilly may have told Dan about her time with Oscar Bates, one would guess that he would have been a suspect were he not conducting the murder investigation. I knew more of what was going on during that time than most everyone, and I hated the SOB Bates for grabbing my you-know-whats, and all of the hate he had for my family. Devine never considered me a murder suspect or asked me any questions about that night. The murder is listed in police files as unsolved to this day. Someone, or maybe two people, got away with the killing of Bates, who knows? I may never say who I think did the deed.

"At times, citizens do things that government people find unable to accomplish. Ya know, Sally, while at the club, I learned lots about life, and especially the value of family, especially in a wealthy modern country like ours. These college years have given me a prospective into government, be it local or national, as to its considerable power and value for everyone so long as it remembers where the most important foundation for all of us lies."

"John, you should be a politician."

"I hope not. No, I developed these ideas from my government classes and by, on my own, reading about our founders, Washington, Adams, Jefferson, Hamilton, Madison, and Abe, and others like the Englishman Locke. Their ideas go way back to the Greeks and the Roman Empire days of Hadrian, and even Cicero at the time of the Republic.

"My readings taught me that when government gets to a point where it believes itself to be necessary for just about all policies and ideas, then it can become a destructive force. It can dampen creativity of its citizens. I experienced a little of that in my teens and didn't appreciate or understand what was happening.

"Aggressive government can start to protect itself from its citizens and use its powerful position of authority to benefit itself. That is when it starts, slowly, to destroy the most necessary part of our, or any, country, by undermining the family. As Madison so wonderfully pointed out, government is necessary but only so much of it. I realize that point of just so much government is always up for discussion, especially in a complicated country like the USA.

"But if one is looking for love, common sense, unconditional acceptance, guidance, and good values and protecting one's back, then I will rely on my family above government, always."

"John Boy—"

"Sally, stop that Boy stuff."

"Okay, but I know you are not telling me everything. You're smart. You always told me that you kept your eyes and ears open. Come on, what happened the night Bates went down? You know who did it, don't you!"

"Sally, I'll be open and as honest as I can. I do know what happened."

"How!"

"It was Dan who met Bates at the outhouse. He was there just to have it out because he honestly believed that Bates did have sex with his wife, Lilly. He wanted to beat the hell out of him and more, just break his legs so he would never walk again. He told me more than I wanted to know."

"Then what happened? How do you know so much?"

"I was there."

"What! You were there?"

"Yes, I was there, and very, very close."

"You hit him with the Volmer bat."

"No more. That is as far as I will go. End of story."

The End

ABOUT THE AUTHOR

JOHN MICHELE GREW up in a multi-cultural ethnic neighborhood north of Boston, Massachusetts, in the three-decker home of his grandparents. In his words, "It was my Rose Garden. It was where I realized early on that honest effort will make a positive difference in one's future".

He began a career in finance and banking, first as a teller, and rose to organize a newly chartered bank in Southern New Hampshire, where he served as Chairman, President, and CEO. The bank grew to twelve locations and became a publicly traded company listed on NASDAQ before it merged into a large Boston Institution. After the merger, he served as President of its New Hampshire operations. He is a graduate of Northeastern University and the School of Banking at Williams College. He also served as an advisory board member of the Whittemore School of Business and Economics at the University of New Hampshire. He resides in Bedford, New Hampshire.

He enjoys gardening, growing fig-trees, and loves fly fishing, especially for Atlantic Salmon and trout. When fortunate to catch one, he will return it to the stream. When one catches a salmon, it is the fisherman who is caught. He also enjoys building dry stone walls.

He is most proud of his four children and eight grandchildren, their husbands and wives, all of whom are talented, handsome, and beautiful. Equally important, they all possess excellent caring characters.

CPSIA information can be obtained
at www.ICGtesting.com
Printed in the USA
LVHW030342070821
694695LV00002B/302

9 781662 443978